Disney's Storybook

COLLECTION

Disney's Storybook COLLECTION

SCHOLASTIC INC.

New York   Toronto   London   Auckland   Sydney
Mexico City   New Delhi   Hong Kong

TABLE OF CONTENTS

TABLE OF CONTENTS

ISBN 0-439-15325-5

Copyright © 1998 by Disney Enterprises, Inc.
All rights reserved.
Published by Scholastic Inc., 555 Broadway, New York, NY 10012,
by arrangement with Disney Press, an imprint of Buena Vista Books, Inc.
SCHOLASTIC and associated logos are trademarks and/or registered trademarks of Scholastic Inc.

12 11 10 9 8 7 6 5 4 3 2   1 2 3 4/0

Printed in the U.S.A.   24

First Scholastic printing, November 1999

The edition containing *Bambi, A Life in the Woods*
by Felix Salten is published by Simon & Schuster.

101 Dalmations is based on the original book by Dodie Smith,
published by Viking Press.

This book is set in 20-point Cochin.

Edited by Nancy Parent
Designed by Todd Taliaferro

WALT DISNEY'S

Snow White
and the Seven Dwarfs

Long ago, in a faraway place, there lived a lovely princess named Snow White. Her hair was black as coal, her lips red as rose, and her skin as white as snow.

Snow White's stepmother, the Queen, was very cruel.

She hated anyone who was more beautiful than she. The Queen treated Snow White like a servant.

Snow White never complained. She was obedient and hard-working, but she dreamed of a handsome prince who would take her away to his castle. One day, while drawing water from the well, a handsome stranger did appear, charmed by Snow White's singing. But Snow

White was too shy to speak to him.

Inside the castle, the Queen asked her magic mirror, "Mirror, mirror, on the wall, who is the fairest one of all?"

Every day the mirror had the same reply. "You are the fairest," he told her. And the Queen was content for another day.

But as Snow White grew older, she also grew more

beautiful. And the Queen became very jealous.

One day the magic mirror told the Queen that someone else was the fairest in the land. It was the princess, Snow White!

In a jealous rage, the Queen called her royal huntsman into the throne room.

"Take Snow White far into the forest and kill her," she commanded. "And as proof of your deed, bring me back her heart in this." She handed the stunned huntsman a beautiful carved box.

"Poor Snow White," said the hunter to the innocent princess. "I cannot kill you. You must run away and hide from the Queen!"

Snow White was so frightened that she ran off through the dark woods.

At last she came to a cottage. "Who lives here?" Snow White wondered.

Then she heard voices singing in the distance. The seven dwarfs who lived in the cottage were coming home from a hard day at work in the diamond mine.

The dwarfs introduced themselves. Their names were Sleepy, Grumpy, Happy, Doc, Dopey, Sneezy, and Bashful.

They invited Snow White to share their supper.

Snow White felt so safe with the dwarfs that she decided to stay with them.

But the evil queen soon found out that Snow White was still alive. She would have to take matters into her own wicked hands.

She fled to the dungeon beneath the castle. There the Queen mixed a potion that would change her into an old hag. Then she took an apple and slowly dipped it into another potion. "One bite of this poisoned apple and Snow White will close her eyes forever!" she cackled.

The old woman appeared at Snow White's window. "Hello, dearie," she said. "Taste one of my delicious apples. It's apple pies that make menfolk's mouths water. Pies made from apples like these." Then she held the poisoned apple out to Snow White.

The birds tried to warn Snow White away from the poisoned fruit. They fluttered and flew around the hag, trying to make her drop the apple.

"Stop it! Stop it!" cried Snow White.

The birds flew away sadly. Then the animals of the forest ran to the dwarfs to warn them that something was very wrong and they needed to come right home!

The seven dwarfs raced to the cottage and found the old woman trying to sneak away and Snow White lying lifeless on the floor. The dwarfs chased the hag into the forest.

A storm began to blow as the evil woman ran away. Suddenly she came to the edge of a steep and rocky cliff.

First, she tried to move a huge rock so it would roll down on top of the poor dwarfs and crush them.

"Look out!" cried Grumpy to the others.

At that moment, lightning struck. The Queen lost her balance and fell to her doom!

The sad little dwarfs built a bed of gold and glass for their beloved Snow White. They kept watch over her, day and night.

Then one day a handsome prince rode into the forest. How beautiful the young woman was! The Prince knelt down and kissed Snow White tenderly.

His kiss awakened her. Then Snow White and the Prince rode off to his kingdom, where they lived happily ever after.

WALT DISNEY'S

Pinocchio

Once upon a time, Geppetto the woodcarver made a special puppet that he named Pinocchio. "I wish you were a real boy," said Geppetto, sadly.

That night the Blue Fairy came to Geppetto's

workshop. "Good Geppetto," she said, "you have made others so happy, you deserve to have your wish come true."

Smiling, the Blue Fairy touched the puppet gently with her wand. "Little puppet made of pine, wake! The gift of life be thine!" And in the blink an an eye, she brought Pinocchio to life.

"Pinocchio, if you are brave, truthful, and unselfish, you will be a real boy someday," said the Blue Fairy.

Then she turned to Jiminy Cricket. "Jiminy," she said, "you must help Pinocchio." She told Jiminy that she was giving him a very important job. He must be Pinocchio's conscience—keeper of the knowledge of right and wrong.

The next day Geppetto proudly sent his little wooden boy off to school. "Jiminy Cricket will show you the way," said Geppetto. "Be sure to go right there!"

Pinocchio headed off, but never found his way to

school. He went away with Stromboli, an evil puppeteer, who promised to make him famous. That night Pinocchio had great fun as he danced on the stage. But afterward Stromboli locked him in a cage so he could never escape.

The Blue Fairy appeared and asked Pinocchio why he

hadn't gone to school. Pinocchio lied and told her he had

been kidnapped. Suddenly his nose began to grow.

When Pinocchio finally told the truth, the fairy set him

free. "I'll forgive you this once, Pinocchio. But this is the last

time I can help you. Remember, a boy who won't be good

might just as well be made of wood!"

The next day Pinocchio met a man who drove a stagecoach pulled by a team of sad little donkeys. "Come with us to Pleasure Island!" said the coachman. The stagecoach was full of noisy boys. They were laughing and talking all at once. Pinocchio thought it looked like fun.

"Don't go, Pinoke!" cried Jiminy Cricket, but still Pinocchio climbed aboard, ready for adventure.

On Pleasure Island, Pinocchio and the other boys ran wild and stuffed themselves with sweets. But Pinocchio's fun did not last long. All of a sudden, he began to grow donkey ears and a tail!

Pinocchio was frightened. He and Jiminy Cricket ran for their lives, away from Pleasure Island.

But when the two returned home, Geppetto was gone. Pinocchio was very upset. Where could Geppetto be? A dove suddenly appeared with a note from Geppetto. The note said he had gone to sea to look for Pinocchio and had been swallowed by a whale.

Pinocchio set off at once to find Monstro the whale and save his father. And indeed, Pinocchio found Geppetto in the belly of the great whale. Geppetto was thrilled to see his little puppet. But how were they ever going to get out of there? Pinocchio had an idea. Together, they built a fire and used the smoke to make Monstro sneeze.

Geppetto and Pinocchio were thrown out of the whale and into the sea. Fighting the waves, Pinocchio helped get his father to shore safe and sound. But there was

Pinocchio lying facedown in the water! Geppetto

scooped Pinocchio up in his arms and carried him home.

Geppetto laid Pinocchio on his bed and knelt by his side.

"Little Pinocchio, you risked your life to save me," he sobbed.

Suddenly the Blue Fairy appeared once more. Waving

her magic wand over Pinocchio, she said, "Now you have proven yourself brave, truthful, and unselfish. Today you will become a real boy. Awake, Pinocchio, awake!"

Jiminy Cricket watched as his friend came to life. Their troubles were over and Jiminy's job was done. At last, Geppetto's wish for a real son had come true.

WALT DISNEY'S
Bambi

One beautiful spring morning a little rabbit named Thumper woke Friend Owl with some wonderful news. A baby deer had been born deep in the woods. "It's happened!" cried the little rabbit. "A new prince is born!"

"What's his name?" asked the animals.

"Why, his name is Bambi," his mother replied.

Soon Bambi met all the other wonderful animals in the forest. First Mrs. Quail and her babies stopped to say hello. Then Mrs. Opossum and her family, who liked to hang upside down, smiled at Bambi. Next, a mole poked his head out from the ground to wish Bambi a good day.

Even a flock of little bluebirds flew down to greet the young prince.

Bambi made friends with Thumper and a shy little

skunk called Flower. They laughed and played together every day. Soon, at the pond in the meadow, Bambi made another friend—a playful girl fawn named Faline.

Summer and fall passed happily for Bambi. And when the cold winter came, Thumper taught Bambi how to spin and slide on the frozen pond. Bambi had never done anything like this before. "C'mon, it's all right," Thumper told him, gliding across the ice. "The water's stiff!"

Finally winter was over and the spring brought many changes. Bambi had grown into a handsome young buck.

His friends Thumper and Flower had grown up, too. Friend Owl couldn't get over them. He was sure that any moment now they would all meet somebody and become… twitterpated. That meant they would fall in love.

The three friends laughed at the wise old owl and
agreed to spend all their time together—until Flower met
a lovely girl skunk and got twitterpated. Bambi knew he
would miss Flower. But at least he and Thumper could

still spend time together. Then Thumper fell in love, too!

Next it was Bambi's turn. Soon he met a beautiful doe in the meadow. It was his old friend Faline! Bambi suddenly felt dizzy and light as a feather! He was twitterpated. Bambi and Faline frolicked together just as they had done in the meadow when they were young.

But Bambi wasn't the only buck who liked Faline. A stag named Ronno soon pushed his way between them challenging Bambi to a fierce fight. Bambi charged Ronno with all his might and the two bucks butted heads again and again. Finally, Bambi won the fight. And from that day on, he and Faline were always together.

One fall morning Bambi smelled something strange— smoke. Just then a majestic stag appeared. It was Bambi's father, the Great Prince. "The forest is on fire!" he cried. "Hurry! We must warn the other animals to run to the river island."

Bambi and the Prince warned all the forest animals.

Then they crossed the river, where they found Faline waiting for them. Bambi and his friends watched as fire destroyed their forest homes and everything around them.

After the fire was out, the old stag turned to Bambi. "I must leave you now," he said. "You will take my place as

Prince of the Forest." Bambi knew this was a great

responsibility, but he was ready to accept it.

And Bambi knew that when the last bit of smoke was

gone, the animals would bravely rebuild their homes.

Fall once again turned into winter and winter into spring. The forest was lush and green and smelled of blooming flowers.

Soon Thumper and his little bunnies were waking Friend Owl once again. Faline had given birth to twin fawns. All the animals proudly came to celebrate.

But no one was prouder than Bambi, the new Prince

of the Forest. He stood overlooking the thicket, smiling down on his family, his heart filled with love. Soon, Bambi would teach them the lessons of the forest that he himself had learned so long ago.

Walt Disney's Cinderella

Once upon a time, there was a pretty young girl named Cinderella. Cinderella was loved by everyone because she was good and sweet and kind. But Cinderella's widowed father believed she needed a mother. So he married again to a woman with two daughters of her own. Soon Cinderella's father died and she was left to live with her mean stepmother and two jealous stepsisters in the attic of their house.

Poor Cinderella had to do all of the cooking and cleaning. She no longer had nice things and wore only tattered old clothes, while her stepmother and stepsisters had very nice clothes and lived very comfortably.

But no matter how mean her stepmother

and stepsisters were, Cinderella was always cheerful. Even the little animals loved to be near her. She made friends with the mice and birds, making them little outfits to wear and caring for them. Two of Cinderella's best friends were Jaq and Gus. Cinderella and Jaq were always saving Gus from mean old Lucifer the cat, who had his eye on the plump little mouse.

One day a letter came

inviting everyone to the palace for a ball. Cinderella's

stepmother said, "Cinderella may go, but only if she

finishes her work." Cinderella happily washed, ironed,

and scrubbed the floors all day.

Meanwhile, Cinderella's little friends went to work

making her a lovely gown. The birds and mice who loved Cinderella wanted so much to surprise her. And when she saw what they had done, she was very touched. She put on the beautiful dress and ran downstairs to join her stepsisters.

The birds and mice had used sashes and ribbons and beads that belonged to Cinderella's stepsisters to make the dress look nice. But when her stepsisters saw the gown, they tore it to shreds.

"That's my ribbon!" cried one.

"And those are my beads!" yelled the other.

Cinderella ran to the garden in tears. "Now I can't go to the ball!" she cried.

"Don't cry, child," said a gentle voice. "I am your fairy

godmother, and I have come to help you."

Then the Fairy Godmother waved her wand. Four

mice became four proud white horses, and a big, round

pumpkin became a glittering coach.

Again the Fairy Godmother waved her wand and turned Cinderella's torn dress into a beautiful gown. "You must leave the ball by midnight," she warned. "After that, the magic spell will be broken."

At the ball, the Prince danced with Cinderella all evening. She felt as if she were floating on a dream!

The King and the Grand Duke were delighted to see

them falling in love.

But as the clock struck midnight, Cinderella ran from

the palace. She was in such a hurry that she left one glass

slipper behind. The Prince ran after her, but it was too late.

The next day, the Prince sent the Grand Duke door-to-door to find the young woman who had lost her slipper. When they got to Cinderella's house, both stepsisters tried on the glass slipper, but their feet were much too big.

Cinderella's stepmother told the Grand Duke that there were no other ladies in the house. She had locked Cinderella in her room upstairs on purpose. But Cinderella's little friends Gus and Jaq stole the key from her stepmother's pocket, opened her door, and freed Cinderella just in time.

When Cinderella appeared and asked if she could try on the slipper, her stepmother was furious. She tripped the footman who was holding the slipper on a pillow.

It fell to the floor and shattered.

But Cinderella reached into her apron pocket and pulled out the matching one. It was a perfect fit!

The Grand Duke was happy and relieved that he had found the slipper's owner. The Prince would be married at last. And Cinderella's dreams would all come true.

WALT DISNEY'S

ALICE
in
WONDERLAND

One beautiful spring day a young girl named Alice sat by the river listening to her sister read aloud from a history book. But Alice wasn't really listening. She was playing with her cat, Dinah, and daydreaming.

The sun was bright and the air was warm. Soon Alice began to close her eyes. She no longer heard her sister's voice.

Suddenly a large white rabbit dashed by. Alice jumped up. The rabbit was wearing a waistcoat and bow tie and was carrying a huge pocket watch. "I'm late! I'm late for a very important date," the White Rabbit muttered as he went along.

Alice went chasing after him, but stopped short at a rabbit hole.

The rabbit scuttled down the hole. Thinking he might

be late for something fun, like a party, Alice followed him.

Suddenly she stumbled and fell head over heels into the hole. But instead of falling faster, she began falling slower and slower—until she was floating.

She landed gently, just in time to see the rabbit disappear through a tiny door. Alice was too big to follow him. The Doorknob suggested she try the bottle on the table, which said "drink me." Alice drank and drank. With every sip, she got smaller and smaller.

When she was ready to open the door, the Doorknob told her that he was locked. Then he suggested she try a cookie from the box labeled "eat me." Alice did and she began to grow. Soon she was crying giant tears. The Doorknob told her to drink again. She grew smaller and smaller until she could float right through the keyhole.

On the other side of the keyhole, Alice found she was in the strangest place. There were talking birds and walking fish, and a Cheshire cat who kept appearing and disappearing.

Alice kept hoping that one of these creatures could help her find the White Rabbit, but they were no help at all.

She came upon a pair of twins. They introduced

themselves as Tweedledum and Tweedledee.

"How do you do, Tweedledum and Tweedledee?" Alice greeted them. She could not tell them apart at all.

"When first meeting someone, you should shake hands and state your name and business," said Tweedledum, grabbing Alice's hand and shaking it firmly.

"That's manners!" said Tweedledee, grabbing her other hand and giving it a good squeeze.

With that, the twins danced Alice around and around. But they were so rough that they flipped her over, knocking her onto her back. Alice was not pleased.

"Talk about manners!" Alice exclaimed as she picked

herself up. "If you must know, my name is Alice, and I'm following the White Rabbit. I'm very sorry, but I must go."

Despite the twins'

protests, Alice went on her way. Soon she came to an unusual garden. Flying about were bread-and-butterflies and a rocking-horse fly. Alice discovered that the flowers of Wonderland could speak!

"What kind of flower are you?" a big orchid asked her.

"Oh, I'm not any kind of flower," Alice replied.

"Why, no fragrance at all," added another flower, sniffing her. Alice did not know what to make of this.

"Just as I suspected!" a rose cried. "She's nothing but a common weed!" The rose turned her back on Alice.

"Leave!" shouted the flowers. "We don't want you in our lovely garden." They pointed to the way out.

Feeling very upset, Alice was forced to run away.

Then, nearby, Alice saw a familiar grin up in a tree. It was the Cheshire Cat. She asked if he'd seen the White Rabbit.

"No," replied the cat. "But if I were looking for him, I'd ask the Mad Hatter." And with that, the cat began to disappear.

Alice realized that the cat hadn't told her how to find the Mad Hatter. She walked along and saw two road signs pointing in the same direction. One read "Mad Hatter" and the other read "March Hare."

She followed the signs to a clearing in the woods where the Mad Hatter was giving a tea party with the

March Hare. They made Alice feel quite unwelcome. They refused to offer her a cup of tea and had no intention of helping her find the White Rabbit.

Alice went on her way and soon ran into the Cheshire Cat again. She explained that she was trying to find her way home. But the cat replied that all ways led to the Queen. He opened a door and Alice stepped through.

The White Rabbit hurried into view. He was about to announce the Queen! The Queen of Hearts appeared and invited Alice to play croquet. But during their game, the Cheshire Cat showed up and tripped Her Royal Majesty. The Queen was enraged and blamed Alice. "Off with her head!" she cried. There was a mad chase and Alice ran through Wonderland to get away.

Suddenly Alice awoke on the riverbank. "You've been

dreaming," her sister said.

Alice looked around but didn't see any strange talking creatures. All she saw were her sister, the old history book, and Dinah, her kitten. And that was just fine with Alice.

Walt Disney's Peter Pan

Long ago, in the city of London, there lived a family named Darling. Wendy, John, and Michael Darling would sit in the nursery telling stories about a far-off place called Never Land where the daring Peter Pan and the pixie Tinker Bell lived. And no one in Never Land ever grew old.

Peter Pan and Tinker Bell came to the Darlings' nursery window one night to get his shadow. It wasn't Peter's first visit to the Darling house. He had come there many times to listen to Wendy's stories. Peter was upset when Wendy explained that this was to be her last night in the nursery.

"But that means no more stories," cried Peter, "unless I take you all back to Never Land with me."

"That would be wonderful," the children shouted. Everyone but Tinker Bell agreed.

"But how will we get there?" Wendy asked.

"All you've got to do is fly," Peter replied.

And, with a sprinkle of pixie dust from Tinker Bell, they soared through the skies of London and all the way to Peter's Never Land home.

Down below they saw waterfalls and Mermaid Lagoon. There was a pirate ship, a forest, and even an Indian camp.

The pirate ship belonged to a fellow called Captain Hook. The captain had two enemies in Never Land—Peter

Pan and a hungry crocodile. One day, in a fight with Peter,

the crocodile had gotten a taste of Hook's hand and had

followed him around ever since, hoping for more. Hook

blamed Peter Pan.

When they got to Never Land, Peter took Wendy,

Michael, and John into the forest to meet the Lost Boys.

Then he and Wendy went to visit Mermaid Lagoon.

There Peter spied the Indian Chief's daughter, Tiger Lily,

tied up in Captain Hook's boat. They heard Hook ask

Tiger Lily to reveal Peter's hiding place. But the Indian princess wouldn't tell him anything.

"I have to save Tiger Lily!" Peter cried. He and Wendy followed Hook to Skull Rock. Peter challenged the Captain to a duel. But Peter was too fast and too smart for Hook. With one quick lunge, the Captain landed in the water next to his greatest fear—the hungry crocodile.

Peter rescued Tiger Lily and brought her back to the Indian camp.

Captain Hook got away from the crocodile and swore revenge against Peter Pan. He kidnapped Tinker

Bell and tricked her into telling him where Peter lived.

Then the pirates went to Peter's hideout and captured

Wendy, John, Michael, and the Lost Boys.

Knowing that Peter would never be able to resist a beautifully wrapped package, the pirates left a present in the tree house for him. As soon as he opened it, BOOM, it would explode! And that would be the end of Peter Pan.

Tinker Bell knew what Hook had planned. She had to warn Peter before it was too late! She made her escape carefully and flew back to the hideout.

"Peter Pan will save us," Wendy insisted as she was

about to walk the plank.

But the evil captain just laughed at her. "Pan will never save you now!" he cried with glee.

Captain Hook did not realize that Tinker Bell was

already on her way to get Peter.

Peter and Tinker Bell returned in a flash. "Hook, this

time you've gone too far!" Peter shouted as he challenged him to one last duel.

Wendy, Michael, John, and the Lost Boys watched in awe as Peter fought so bravely to save them. At last Hook and the pirates ended up in the water. They swam as fast as they could, with the always-hungry crocodile close behind.

"Thank you so much for saving us," said Wendy. "And now I think it's time for us to go back home."

Before they could say "Captain Hook," Peter set sail in Hook's very own ship through the skies of Never Land.

They were soon back in London safe and sound.

Peter and Tinker Bell said their good-byes, and the Darlings promised never to forget the wonderful times they had. As the years went by, they would remember everything — Peter, Tinker Bell, the Pirates, Tiger Lily, and the Lost Boys — just as if it had all happened yesterday.

WALT DISNEY'S

Lady and the TRAMP

Lady was a happy little dog. She lived in a big house with Jim Dear and Darling. One day Lady learned that Darling was expecting a baby. Lady didn't know that things in the house would soon be very different.

One day Lady met a scruffy dog named Tramp. Tramp had no home and no family. He went wherever he pleased and did whatever he pleased.

"Believe me," Tramp told Lady and her friends Jock and Trusty, "babies change everything! Now you'll have nothing but trouble. Just wait and see!"

But Tramp was wrong. When the baby arrived, Lady had one more wonderful person to care for and love.

Several weeks later, Jim Dear and Darling went off on a trip. Aunt Sarah came to stay at the house. "Lady," said Jim Dear, "help Aunt Sarah take care of the baby."

Aunt Sarah brought her Siamese cats with her. They

made a lot of trouble. Lady barked at the cats, but it did no good.

"Shame on you, Lady!" shouted Aunt Sarah. "Attacking my poor little angels. A muzzle is what you need!" She took Lady right to the pet shop to buy one.

The muzzle was more than Lady could bear. She had to run away. When Lady stopped to catch her breath, she was in a strange part of town surrounded by a pack of mean dogs. Just then her friend Tramp appeared. Seeing that Lady was in danger, he fought the stray dogs and chased them off.

"You poor kid!" said Tramp, looking at the muzzle. He took Lady to the zoo, where a friendly beaver chewed right through the muzzle and freed Lady.

Afterward, Tramp took Lady to visit one of his favorite places. They shared a romantic dinner for two at Tony's Italian restaurant.

Finally, after a lovely stroll through the park, Lady said, "I must go home. I promised Jim Dear I'd take care of the baby."

"Okay, Pigeon," said Tramp. "But let's have some fun first."

"Tramp, no!" said Lady. But Tramp had already rushed into a nearby yard to chase the squawking chickens.

Suddenly the dogcatcher appeared. Before she knew it, Lady was on her way to the pound without Tramp. Lady was ashamed and scared in the pound—especially when the other dogs began to tease her. A dog named Peg came to Lady's rescue. "Can't ya see the poor kid's scared enough already?" Peg said to the other dogs.

The dogs were jealous because Lady had a shiny license and would soon be going home.

When Lady finally came home, Tramp said, "I'm sorry I got you in trouble, Pidge." But Lady was too angry to listen. She refused to speak to Tramp.

Later that night, Lady saw a rat scurry up a vine to the baby's room. She barked as loudly as she could.

When Tramp heard Lady barking, he came running.

"What's wrong, Pidge?" he asked.

When Lady told him about the rat, Tramp ran into the

house and up the stairs.

Lady pulled at her chain until it broke. Then she ran up to the baby's room to help Tramp fight the rat and save the baby.

"You vicious brutes!" cried Aunt Sarah when she saw Lady and Tramp in the baby's room. "Get away from the baby!"

Aunt Sarah called the dogcatcher to come and take Tramp away.

When Jim Dear and Darling came home that night, Lady helped Jim Dear find the dead rat.

"Lady," said Jim Dear thankfully, "I think you and your friend were trying to save our baby from the rat."

Meanwhile, Jock and Trusty went to find Tramp. They soon caught up with the dogcatcher's wagon. Trusty began barking very loudly—so loudly, in fact, that he

scared the horses. They reared up and the wagon tipped

over right onto poor Trusty.

Trusty had a broken leg, but he would be just fine.

Lady and Jim Dear arrived just in time to free Tramp.

Jim Dear and Darling were so grateful to Tramp that they asked him to live with them always.

By Christmas of that year, Lady and Tramp had four puppies—and the family's happiness was complete.

WALT DISNEY'S

Sleeping Beauty

Long ago, in a faraway kingdom, a tiny princess was born. Her parents, the King and Queen, named her Aurora. Her parents announced that Aurora would one day marry young Prince Phillip. He lived in a neighboring kingdom.

To celebrate Aurora's birth, the King held a great feast at the castle. People came from near and far, bringing gifts for the child.

Three good fairies came to the feast, and they brought the baby special gifts.

"Mine shall be the gift of beauty," said the first good fairy. "Mine shall be the gift of song," said the second.

Before the third good fairy could speak, an evil witch named Maleficent appeared. She was angry because she hadn't been invited to the feast.

Maleficent warned that on Aurora's sixteenth birthday, the girl would prick her finger on a spinning wheel and die.

But the third good fairy had not yet spoken. "No, the Princess will not die!" she said quickly. "She will only sleep—until true love's kiss breaks the spell."

To keep Aurora safe, the King and Queen secretly sent her to live with the good fairies. The fairies called the child Briar Rose so that no one would

know who she was.

On the day of Briar Rose's sixteenth birthday, the

fairies sent her off to pick berries in the woods. Then they began preparing for her birthday party.

The fairies had put away their magic for fear that they would be discovered by Maleficent. But after struggling with a lopsided cake and a dress that just didn't look right, they retrieved their magic wands and set about making everything perfect for Briar Rose.

Meanwhile, beautiful Briar Rose wandered through the woods with her animal friends. Suddenly a handsome young man appeared. Briar Rose did not know it was Prince Phillip.

Later that day, when the birthday celebration was over, it was time for the Princess to return to the castle. She was going to live with her parents once again.

That night the evil fairy Maleficent appeared at the castle and lured Aurora away to a lonely tower. There she tricked the Princess into touching a spinning wheel. Aurora pricked her finger and fell into a deep sleep.

To save the King and Queen from terrible heartache, the good fairies put everyone in the castle to sleep.

Meanwhile, Maleficent wanted to keep Prince Phillip away from Aurora, so she locked the Prince in a dungeon.

Phillip was not a prisoner for long. The good fairies brought him a magic shield and sword. Soon he was on his way to rescue the Princess.

To keep Prince Phillip from entering the castle, Maleficent surrounded it with thick branches full of thorns. But that didn't stop the Prince.

As the Prince came closer to the castle, Maleficent turned herself into an angry dragon.

It was a terrible fight, but Phillip used his magic shield

and sword and finally defeated the dragon.

Prince Phillip raced to the tower and found the sleeping

beauty. He kissed her tenderly, and the Princess awoke.

At the same moment, everyone in the castle awoke. The

King and Queen were overjoyed to see their daughter again.

Soon it was announced that Princess Aurora and Prince Phillip would marry. Everyone in the kingdom rejoiced, for they knew that Aurora and her prince would live happily ever after.

Walt Disney's

101 DALMATIANS

Pongo, Perdita, and their fifteen puppies lived in a cozy little house in London. The house belonged to their humans, Roger and Anita. They were perfectly happy until they met Cruella De Vil—Anita's old schoolmate who simply loved spotted puppies.

She wanted to buy them all and make them into spotted fur coats!

Roger put his foot down. "These puppies are not for sale and that's final."

Cruella was furious but she refused to give up.

One night Cruella's two nasty henchmen, Horace and

Jasper, kidnapped the puppies! Then they drove out to Cruella's old country estate and waited to hear from their boss.

When the puppies got there, they saw lots and lots of other Dalmatian puppies who had also been snatched by Horace and Jasper.

Back at home, Pongo and Perdita could not believe what had happened.

Perdita knew

at once that Cruella was behind her missing puppies.

"She has stolen them," sobbed Perdita. "Oh, Pongo, do you think we'll ever find them?"

Pongo knew that the Twilight Bark was their only hope. He would bark his message to the dogs in London.

They would pick it up and pass it along to the dogs in the country. And maybe someone would find the puppies.

That night the Twilight Bark reached a quiet farm where an old English sheepdog known as Colonel lay sleeping peacefully.

"Alert, alert!" shouted Sergeant Tibs, a cat who lived on the farm. "Vital message coming in from London."

The Colonel listened closely. "Fifteen puppies have been stolen!" he cried.

Sergeant Tibs remembered hearing barking at the old De Vil place. They headed straight for the gloomy mansion.

The Colonel helped Tibs look through the window. Sure enough, there were the fifteen puppies—plus their eighty-four new friends!

Tibs and the Colonel overheard Cruella, Jasper, and

Horace talking. When they heard her plans to make coats

out of the puppies, they knew there was no time to waste.

The Colonel ran off to get word to Pongo and Perdita

while Tibs helped the puppies escape!

As soon as Horace and Jasper realized what was

happening, they tried to stop the puppies. But it was too late. Pongo and Perdita arrived and fought off the foolish thugs as the puppies hurried to safety.

Once all the dogs were safely out of the house, they

thanked the Colonel and Tibs and went on their way. A black Labrador retriever arranged for them to ride to London in the back of a moving van that was being repaired. The dogs waited in a blacksmith's shop.

Suddenly Cruella's big car drove up the street. She had followed their tracks and was parked and waiting.

But Pongo had a clever idea. There were ashes in the

fireplace. If they all rolled in them, they would be disguised in black soot. Then they could get aboard the van without Cruella

realizing it was them! And that's just what they did.

It worked perfectly until a glob of snow dripped onto a puppy and washed off a patch of soot. From her car, Cruella could see it was a Dalmatian puppy.

"They're escaping!" she cried as the van took off.

There was a really scary chase. Cruella tried to pass the van on the road, but she ended up crashing through a barricade and driving right into a huge pile of snow. Cruella's beautiful car was a wreck! And that wasn't all.

She had lost the puppies! Cruella threw a tantrum.

Pongo and Perdita and 99 puppies arrived home safely, much to Roger and Anita's delight. Roger pulled out a handkerchief and wiped Pongo's face clean.

"What will we do with all these puppies?" Anita asked.

"We'll keep them," Roger answered. He sat down at the piano and composed a song right on the spot. "We'll buy a big place in the country, and we'll have a plantation," he sang. "A Dalmatian plantation!"

And that's exactly what they did.

WALT DISNEY'S
The JungleBook

Long ago, deep in the jungles of faraway India, there lived a wise black panther named Bagheera. One day, as Bagheera sat in a tree, he saw something surprising. "Why, it's a Man-cub!" said the panther.

Bagheera was not able to care for the Man-cub, so he took the baby to live with a family of wolves.

The wolves named the little boy Mowgli and raised him as one of their own.

Ten rainy seasons came and went. Mowgli grew, and

no Man-cub was happier than he. The creatures of the

jungle were good to him.

But one jungle animal did not wish Mowgli well. It was Shere Khan, the strong and cunning tiger.

Shere Khan feared nothing but Man's gun and Man's fire. He was sure the Man-cub would grow up to be a hunter.

"Shere Khan has returned to our part of the jungle!" Akela the wolf said one day. "Surely he will try to kill the boy." Mowgli was no longer safe.

"It is time for Mowgli to return to his own kind," Bagheera said. "I will take him to the Man village."

"Hurry," Akela said. "There is no time to lose."

Bagheera and Mowgli started on their way.

"We'll spend the night here," Bagheera said as they settled down on the branch of a tree.

Just then Kaa the snake appeared. He thought Mowgli would make a tasty morsel. The snake used his hypnotic eyes to put Mowgli in a trance. He wrapped the Man-cub in his coils.

Bagheera awoke just in time to smack Kaa on the head

and send him on his way. It was time to keep moving!

Mowgli decided he didn't want to go with Bagheera. "The jungle is my home!" the Man-cub insisted. He went off on his own.

Along the way Mowgli saw a parade of elephants. He thought it was wonderful and wanted to march along with them. But when it came time for the elephant inspection, Colonel Hathi took a closer look at Mowgli.

"What happened to your trunk?" asked the Colonel.

"Why—you're a Man-cub!" he cried.

Bagheera came to Mowgli's rescue. He insisted on

taking him to the Man village, but Mowgli refused once

more. "Then from now on, you're on your own!" Bagheera told him.

Mowgli soon met a good-natured bear named Baloo. Baloo helped Mowgli forget his troubles. They played together, swam together, and ate sweet, ripe bananas and coconuts all day long.

As the two friends floated on the river, a group of monkeys swooped down on Mowgli. They picked him up and dragged him off to the ancient city of the monkey king.

The monkey king wanted
something from Mowgli.
"Teach me the secret
of fire," King Louie
demanded. "Then
I can be human
like you!"

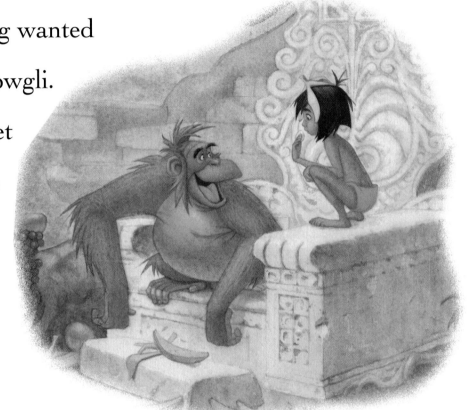

Bagheera and
Baloo arrived in time
to help Mowgli escape from the monkeys. "Now you see
why you must leave the jungle!" they pleaded.

But Mowgli still did not believe his friends. He ran away

from them again—right into the great Shere Khan himself.

"I'm not afraid of you, Shere Khan!" said Mowgli bravely. A storm began to blow around them. Suddenly a bolt of lightning struck nearby.

The lightning started a small fire. Mowgli grabbed a burning branch and tied it to Shere Khan's tail. The terrified tiger ran away, never to be seen again.

As Mowgli proudly walked through the jungle with his friends, he heard a new and beautiful sound. It was a girl from the Man village, singing a sweet song.

Mowgli couldn't look away. He stopped walking to listen. "Go on, Mowgli!" Bagheera urged. "Go on!"

Mowgli knew that he must follow the girl and her song. She smiled at Mowgli as he walked with her all the way to the village. He turned to wave good-bye to his friends.

Baloo and Bagheera watched Mowgli leave. Their hearts were sad, but they knew it was as it should be. Their Man-cub had found his true home at last.

Disney's

THE ARISTOCATS

Madame Bonfamille and her amazing Aristocats lived in a beautiful house in Paris. There were Marie, Toulouse, Berlioz, and Duchess, their mama. The kittens were very talented. Madame loved them very much and planned to leave her entire fortune to them.

Madame did not keep the fact about her fortune a secret. And her wishes did not make Edgar the butler very happy. So Edgar came up with a plan of his own. He would make the Aristocats disappear so he could inherit Madame's fortune!

For supper that very evening, Edgar prepared a special dish.

"Come taste this delicious creme de la creme à la Edgar!" he called.

Unfortunately, it was very delicious. The Aristocats and their friend Roquefort the mouse ate it all. They soon fell fast asleep.

Following his plan, Edgar put them in a basket and

drove them out into the country. He soon met two noisy

dogs who loved to chase anything on wheels. Edgar lost control of his motorcycle and drove right into a river.

The basket holding the Aristocats fell off the motorcycle and under a bridge. When the cats awoke, they did not know where they were. How would they find their way home?

Soon Thomas O'Malley, the alley cat, found the Aristocats and offered his help. He was quite taken with Duchess.

O'Malley arranged a ride aboard a milk truck. But the cats were discovered and chased off the truck.

Concerned for their safety, O'Malley decided to accompany the Aristocats back to Paris. After the very long walk, O'Malley convinced Duchess to stop at his place and rest before going home to Madame.

But when they got to O'Malley's place, his jazz-playing

friends were singing and dancing up a storm. And the Aristocats wanted to meet them all, especially Scat Cat. The kittens joined in the fun, but soon it was time to go home. O'Malley tried to talk Duchess into staying with him, but she was too worried about Madame.

O'Malley agreed to take the Aristocats home. He no sooner saw them to their door when Roquefort came running after him. "Duchess needs help!" cried the little mouse. "Come quickly!"

When Edgar saw the Aristocats, he grabbed them and stuffed them inside a pillowcase. Then he hid them in the oven while he pulled out a huge trunk stamped

"Timbuktu."

O'Malley sent
Roquefort to get
Scat Cat and his
friends and bring
them to Madame's.
Then he ran back to
the house to help
Duchess. He
cornered Edgar in
the barn and there
was a terrible fight.

Edgar pinned poor O'Malley to the wall with a pitchfork!

Suddenly Scat Cat and his friends were at the barn

door. They managed to overpower Edgar. As Roquefort

popped open the trunk to let the Aristocats out, the

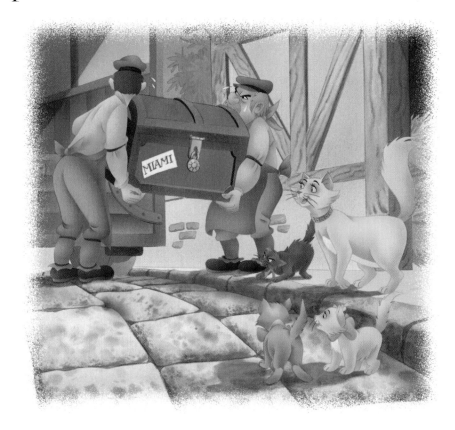

animals made sure that Edgar took their place inside. A few minutes later, some men came to pick up the trunk headed for Timbuktu.

There was the happiest of reunions with Madame! She could not believe her precious cats were home safe and sound. And Madame had Thomas O'Malley and his friends to thank for it.

Madame could see that O'Malley and Duchess were in love. She invited him to live with them. Now her family was complete. And as for O'Malley's musician friends, Madame threw a great party and invited them all to play!

Disney's

—MICKEY'S—
CHRISTMAS CAROL

It was Christmas Eve. But old Ebenezer Scrooge didn't care that it was the best holiday of the year! Poor Bob Cratchit, who worked for Scrooge, had to ask if he could have Christmas Day off. It took all of Cratchit's courage to face his mean boss.

"Christmas!" shouted the miserly Scrooge. "Bah, humbug!"

But he gave his permission. Poor Cratchit hurried home to his family before Scrooge could change his mind.

Just then, Scrooge's nephew Fred stopped by. "Come join us for Christmas dinner, Uncle," he offered.

The old man just scowled. "Christmas! Bah, humbug!" was his only reply, as he shooed Fred out the door.

After counting his money, Scrooge left for home. Sinking into his favorite chair after a bit of dinner, Scrooge began to doze off. Suddenly, he sat up with a start!

CLINK-CLANK-CLINK! The ghost of Jacob Marley, Scrooge's dead business partner, was walking toward him in chains, moaning and groaning.

"I was selfish," said the ghost. "As I carry these chains through eternity, so will you, Scrooge!"

"No!" Scrooge cried. "I must be dreaming. It can't be.

Help me, Jacob. Tell me what I must do!"

"Tonight," Marley said, "three spirits will visit you. Listen to them and do as they say."

When the ghost disappeared, Scrooge shook his head. I need sleep, he thought. Perhaps it was a bit of indigestion.

He had just fallen asleep when the alarm clock rang. There on his night table stood a little fellow. "I am the Ghost of Christmas Past," he said. The ghost held out his hand. "I'll take you to a Christmas of long ago." Scrooge and the spirit flew through the air.

They stopped at a house filled with music and laughter and people. There was a holiday party going on.

"Why, that's me, when I was young!" Scrooge sighed.

"There's old Fezziwig. He gave me my first job. And there's my lovely Isabel."

The spirit reminded Scrooge that gold had taken the place of love in his heart. Scrooge turned away. "I don't want to see any more. Please, Spirit, take me home."

Suddenly the alarm rang once more. "I must have been dreaming again," Scrooge said, rubbing his eyes.

"Fee, fi, fo, fum!" yelled a voice. There sat a giant,

surrounded by a huge feast.

"What's all this?" Scrooge demanded.

"It's the food of generosity," the giant explained. "And

that's something you know

nothing about! I'm the

Ghost of Christmas Present.

Come! See what's happening

tonight." Scrooge followed

the ghost to a tiny house.

He looked through the

cracked window. It was

Bob Cratchit's place. "What

a poor dinner they're having," Scrooge said sadly.

Then he asked, "What's wrong with the little lad?"

"Tiny Tim is very ill," said the giant. "He needs good food to make him strong and well. Pay his father more so he can buy his family enough to eat..." The giant's voice faded, and then he was gone.

Suddenly Scrooge heard another voice behind him. "I am the Ghost of Christmas Yet to Come," it said.

Scrooge turned to find himself in a graveyard. "Whose

lonely grave is this?" he asked meekly.

"It belongs to a very rich man," the ghost said, "a man who was so selfish and unkind that he had no friends." The ghost waited for Scrooge's reaction.

Then Scrooge read the name on the stone. He couldn't believe his eyes! It was his very own grave!

"Oh, give me another chance!" cried Scrooge. "Tell me

it's not too late to change my ways."

Scrooge kept pleading with the spirit until he woke up. There he was, alive and well and right in his own bed! Scrooge leaped out of bed with joy. It wasn't too late—he hadn't missed

Christmas, after all. There was time to make up for his past mistakes.

He dressed quickly and rushed outside. First he tossed

bags of money to the men collecting for the poor. Then he promised his nephew he would come to dinner after he made one stop.

Scrooge hurried over to Bob Cratchit's house. He

brought toys for Tiny Tim and the other children and a wonderful Christmas dinner for everyone.

Cratchit and his wife were never more surprised or pleased than by Scrooge's change of heart. Scrooge made a promise to this family that from this day on they would never want for anything. What a Christmas miracle for the Cratchits and for Ebenezer Scrooge!

Tiny Tim had just one thing to say. "God bless us, every one!"

Disney's

OLIVER & Company

Once upon a time in the great big city of New York, a little kitten lived on the busy streets. He was looking for a home. He met a street-smart dog named Dodger, who wanted his help getting sausages from a food cart. The hungry kitten did his part, but Dodger tricked him and ran off with their meal.

Disappointed and hungry, the kitten followed Dodger to a broken-down barge on the river. There he saw Dodger's

gang—Tito the Chihuahua, Francis the bulldog, Einstein the Great Dane, and a lovely hound named Rita. Dodger was busy acting out the day's events and showing off the sausages they were about to have for dinner.

Suddenly there was a loud crash. The little kitten had fallen right through the roof!

The gang laughed and welcomed the kitten to their home. Soon their master, Fagin, walked in the door. Fagin wanted to see what his pals had collected that day. There was nothing but junk in the box. A car horn sounded and made Fagin jump.

"Yikes! It's Sykes," Fagin said worriedly.

Fagin owed Sykes money and did not have a way to repay him. And Sykes was awfully mean. While Fagin begged for more time, Sykes's Dobermans came aboard the barge and began pushing everybody around. When they tried to corner the kitten, he reached out and scratched one of the Dobermans on the nose.

Fagin and his gang were very impressed with the kitten's bravery, and decided to make him one of the gang. At least the kitten had a home for now.

The next day the gang went out to find money for Fagin. Tito saw a limousine and wanted to check it out. He took the kitten with him. But when Tito accidentally hit the car alarm, the gang fled, leaving the poor kitten tangled up inside.

The little kitten didn't know that there was a passenger in the backseat—a little girl named Jenny. She rescued the kitten and told Winston, the driver, to take them home. She wanted to give the kitten something to eat.

At home, Jenny's pampered poodle, Georgette,

resented the little kitten. But Jenny fell in love with him and named him Oliver. She even got him a special collar and identification tag.

Soon Dodger and the gang showed up to rescue Oliver. But Oliver didn't want to leave with his friends. He belonged with Jenny now. The gang didn't know how Oliver felt. They thought they were helping him get away. When they got back to

Fagin's, the dogs realized they had made a mistake.

Fagin saw the fancy collar and Oliver's new Fifth

Avenue address. And to Fagin, Fifth Avenue meant lots

of money. This was his way out with Sykes! He would

contact the owner at Fifth Avenue, tell them that he

found their cat, and ask for a reward. Then he could pay

Sykes back. Fagin was shocked when Jenny showed up

to get Oliver. He could never take money from a little girl.

When Sykes drove up to get his money, he saw that Fagin was letting the little girl go. He was furious. He grabbed Jenny and kidnapped her. "I'm sure someone will pay a nice ransom for you," Sykes said as he sped away.

Fagin and his gang were determined to help Oliver and Georgette get Jenny back. They hopped onto Fagin's scooter and followed the car to Sykes's warehouse. Then the dogs made their way into the warehouse, where they found Jenny tied up in Sykes's office. They were just about to rescue her when Sykes and his Dobermans found them.

Suddenly Fagin drove his scooter into the warehouse, and they all jumped on. Sykes and his dogs followed them. The chase was on! Fagin headed for the subway, sure that Sykes couldn't follow him. But he did!

Fagin drove his scooter onto the subway tracks with Sykes close behind.

Oliver jumped into Sykes's car to make sure Jenny was okay. He bit Sykes's hand until he let the little girl

go. Just as Sykes's
Doberman was about
to get Oliver, the
kitten jumped
out through sunroof.

A train was
coming, and Fagin
managed to steer onto another track. But Sykes's car
crashed into the oncoming train.

Jenny didn't know what had happened to Oliver. She
was terribly worried. Just then Dodger walked up to her
carrying the little kitten by his neck. When Oliver saw

Jenny, he began to purr. Jenny was overjoyed that Oliver was all right.

The very next day was Jenny's birthday. She had a big party at her house. Fagin and the gang were all there. Everyone was happy. But nobody was happier than the little orphan kitten who had finally found a home.

Disney's

THE PRINCE AND THE PAUPER

Once upon a time there was a good and kindly king. He ruled his country with fairness and generosity.

But one day the King became very ill and could no longer watch over his kingdom. His son, the Prince, stayed by his father's bedside, worrying.

The greedy captain of the guards saw this as his chance to rob the King's loyal subjects, since the King was too ill to protect them. Day after day, the Captain and his soldiers filled up the

palace with mountains of gold. Nobody could save the kingdom from the thieving captain, until...

Two peasants wandered near the palace looking for food. One of the paupers, Mickey, looked exactly like the

Prince. Of course, he didn't have fine clothes to wear or live in a fancy palace, but he did have two loyal friends. One was a rather silly fellow called Goofy, and the other was a friendly dog named Pluto.

Mickey and Goofy watched as the Captain of the Guards sped by in the royal coach filled with food. Pluto was so hungry that he chased the coach toward the palace.

"Stop!" Mickey shouted. "Come back!" And he ran off after his dog.

When Mickey got to the palace, a guard waved him in and called him "Your Majesty."

Meanwhile, inside the palace, the real prince was sitting through another boring lesson with Professor Horace. To amuse himself, he took out his peashooter and aimed it at his servant, Donald.

A little later,

there was a loud crash in the hallway. The Prince and the pauper had each hidden in a suit of armor. When they went tottering down the hallway, they crashed into each other. Lifting their helmets, the two stared and stared.

The Prince talked Mickey into changing places, and headed out of the palace.

The Prince made it past the royal guard, but he couldn't fool Mickey's dog Pluto.

When Goofy saw the Prince, he was sure it was Mickey and struck up a conversation. The Prince said hello and ran off.

Back at the palace, Donald brought food to Mickey's room. Mickey reached out for a turkey leg, but Donald grabbed it first.

"I'm checking for poison," he said, biting into a juicy drumstick.

Pretty soon Donald had eaten all the food. Poor Mickey didn't even get a bite.

Next it was time for the royal lessons. Mickey did not fare very well at falconry or horseback riding. But the Prince wasn't doing any better. He had tried to go sledding with the peasants.

The Prince headed for the marketplace, where he saw the Captain of the Guards stealing food from the poor people. He ordered the Captain to stop, but the Captain just looked at the raggedy peasant and laughed.

A few minutes later, the town crier came through the

square with news that the King had died.

"I must go to my palace right away," the Prince said. "I will miss my father greatly, but now it is my duty to take over as king."

"Gosh," said Goofy. "You're the Prince. I thought you

were my buddy Mickey."

"I am your friend from now on," vowed the Prince, rushing off to the palace.

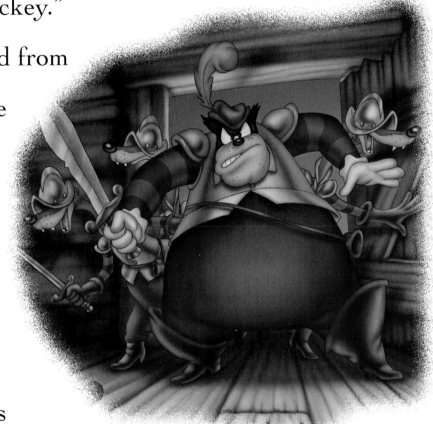

The Captain of the Guards was waiting for His Royal Highness. As soon as the Prince got back to the palace, he was thrown into the dungeon.

"I see your royal ring," the Captain said. "But it won't

do you any good. As soon as the pauper is crowned king, I shall unmask him as an impostor and rule the kingdom myself!"

But the Prince was not alone in the dungeon. Donald was there, too!

Soon a strange-looking guard came to unlock the dungeon door. It was Goofy! He let the Prince out just in time for the coronation.

Meanwhile, Mickey was stalling and trying to avoid being crowned king. "Please don't put it on my head!" Mickey begged.

"He is not the Prince!" yelled the wicked captain. "He's an impostor! Seize him!"

"But *I'm* not an impostor!" came a voice from a high balcony. It was the real prince! There was a huge fight and Mickey, the Prince, and their friends trapped the Captain of the Guards and his soldiers.

Finally the Prince was crowned king. His first act was to arrest the Captain and his men.

Now that the kingdom was once again in kind, caring hands, Mickey was happily reunited with his friends and faithful pup. And the new king was content.

DISNEY'S
THE LITTLE
MERMAID

Once upon a time there was a little mermaid named Ariel who lived in a kingdom under the sea.

Every day Ariel longed for the world above the ocean. "If only I could be a human instead of a mermaid," she said to herself.

Ariel's father, King Triton, found out that Ariel had been swimming to the ocean's surface even though it was forbidden.

"Keep an eye on Ariel," the king ordered the court composer, Sebastian the crab. "Don't let her go near any humans!"

But Sebastian could not stop Ariel. One day she approached a sailing

ship where she spied a
handsome prince
named Eric.

Suddenly a terrible
storm came up. Ariel
saw Prince Eric fall
overboard.

"I've got to save
him!" cried Ariel. She found the Prince and pulled him
to safety.

Before Eric awoke, Ariel sang to him. She thought he
was the most wonderful human she'd ever seen.

Long after Ariel returned to the sea, Eric could hear her beautiful voice in his dreams.

King Triton found out that Ariel had disobeyed him once again. "I told you to stay away from humans!" he shouted.

"But, Daddy, I love him!" Ariel cried. She had to see Prince Eric again.

Later that day, Ariel went to Ursula, the evil sea witch. Ursula promised to turn Ariel into a human—for a price. "You must give me your voice," Ursula commanded. "And if your prince doesn't kiss you in three days, you're mine!"

Ariel agreed to give Ursula her voice. Within seconds,

she had human legs and could no longer swim. Sebastian

and Flounder had to help her to shore.

When the Prince found Ariel, he did not know who

she was. "Can't you speak?" he asked. "Then let me help

you. I'll take you to the palace."

On the second day of Ariel's visit, Prince Eric took her on a tour of his kingdom. They went for a romantic boat ride in the lagoon. But before Eric could kiss her, Ursula's nasty eels overturned the boat.

Ursula knew she needed to take matters into her own tentacles. So she changed herself into a beautiful girl named Vanessa. Ariel's voice was tucked safely inside a shell around Vanessa's neck.

As soon as Eric heard the voice, he became hypnotized. He agreed to marry Vanessa that very day aboard his wedding ship.

Ariel's friend Scuttle the seagull discovered Ursula's trick. He led an army of birds and sea creatures to the ship, hoping to stop the wedding.

In the struggle, Vanessa's necklace shattered. Instantly,

Eric awoke from his spell and Ariel got her voice back. Now she could finally tell Eric who she really was.

But just then, the sun set, and Ariel was turned back into a mermaid. The Sea Witch grabbed her and dived overboard. Eric followed them into the sea. He fought

Ursula with all his strength and wits, and finally

destroyed her.

At last, Ariel was back with her father under the sea.

But she was very unhappy. Now she and her prince

would never be together.

Even King Triton could see how unhappy Ariel really was. "She really loves him, doesn't she?" the king asked Sebastian.

Sebastian nodded yes, and Triton knew what he must

do. The sea king waved his trident, making Ariel human again. Soon, aboard the royal wedding ship, Ariel said good-bye to her friends under the sea. She and her prince were together forever. The Little Mermaid's wish had finally come true.

Disney's

Beauty and the Beast

Once upon a time there was a prince who was so selfish and unkind that he and all who lived in his castle were put under a powerful spell.

The prince was turned into a terrible beast. He would

change back into a prince only if he learned to love

someone and be loved in return.

In a nearby village lived a beautiful young woman

named Belle. She loved to read books about adventure

and romance.

Gaston, the hunter, followed Belle everywhere in town. He wanted to marry her, but Belle thought Gaston was a conceited bully.

One dark winter day, Belle's father, Maurice, started off on a journey through the woods and lost his way. Maurice found shelter in a gloomy castle. There he was greeted by the Beast's servants. The spell had changed them all into enchanted objects.

Before long Maurice was discovered by the Beast!

"What are you staring at?" roared the angry beast.

Then he threw Maurice into a dungeon.

Maurice's horse came home alone. "Where's Papa?"

cried Belle. "Take me to him!" Belle climbed on, and the

horse galloped back to the Beast's castle.

The Beast terrified Belle, but she tried to be brave.

"Let my father go!" she cried. "Let me take his place."

The Beast agreed, but only if Belle promised to stay in his gloomy castle forever.

The Beast's enchanted servants welcomed Belle and tried to make her feel at home. There was Cogsworth the mantel clock, Lumiere the candelabra, and Mrs. Potts the teapot. They knew that if Belle and the Beast fell in love, the spell that lay over the castle would be broken.

Little by little the Beast grew kinder toward Belle.

One day he led her to his magnificent library.

"It's wonderful!" Belle gasped.

"It's yours," said the Beast.

Belle slowly grew fonder of the Beast and learned to

trust him. She even taught him how to dance. But her heart ached for her father. "If only I could see him again," she told the Beast.

"Come with me," he answered. "I will show him to you."

The Beast's rooms showed the effects of his anger and despair. Belle held up a magic mirror and saw Maurice, looking tired and sick.

"I must go to him!" cried Belle.

The Beast agreed to let Belle go, even though it meant the end of his hopes for breaking the spell.

When Belle returned home, she told Gaston about the Beast's kindness. Gaston was jealous.

He convinced the villagers that the Beast was a monster and should be destroyed. He led the angry mob to the Beast's castle.

Gaston found the Beast and fought him on the castle rooftops. In the midst of the battle, Gaston lost his footing and fell to his death—but not before he had stabbed the Beast.

Belle rushed to the Beast's side only to find him badly wounded. "You came back," he whispered.

Belle's tears fell upon the Beast. "I love you," she cried.

The spell was broken! The Beast was transformed into a handsome prince, and the enchanted servants became human once more. Belle and her prince would live very happily ever after.

DISNEY'S

Aladdin

Long ago, in a faraway land called Agrabah, there lived a poor orphan named Aladdin. One day in the market, Aladdin took some bread for his dinner. The Sultan's guards chased him, but Aladdin and his pet monkey, Abu, escaped. Then Aladdin saw two hungry

children and gave the bread to them. "Things will change,"
he promised Abu. "Someday we'll live in a palace!"

That afternoon at the palace, Princess Jasmine was
told by her father, the Sultan, that she must marry a
prince in three days. Jasmine was very unhappy. "I will

marry only for
love!" she cried.

Jasmine told
Rajah, her pet
tiger, that she
would have to
leave the palace.

Disguising herself in an old peasant robe, the Princess ran away. Tired and hungry, Jasmine took an apple from a stall in the market, but couldn't pay the angry fruit seller. Aladdin came to her rescue. The mean merchant called the guards. They released the Princess, but took Aladdin to the palace dungeon.

Meanwhile, Jafar, the Sultan's evil advisor, disguised himself as a prisoner. "Help me find a very special lamp," he said to Aladdin, "and I'll set you free."

Jafar took Aladdin and Abu to the Cave of Wonders. A magic carpet appeared and led Aladdin to the lamp. But just as Aladdin reached for it, Abu grabbed a large, sparkling jewel.

The cave began to collapse. The magic carpet saved Aladdin and Abu, but all three were trapped. "What's so special about this old lamp?" Aladdin wondered aloud. As Aladdin rubbed the dusty lamp, an enormous genie appeared.

"Master," he said, "I can grant you three wishes, but

you can't wish for more wishes. Now let's get out of here!"

Aladdin's first wish was to become a prince so Jasmine would want to marry him. But he promised to save his last wish to set the Genie free.

Later that day, Aladdin arrived at the palace in grand style, introducing himself as Prince Ali Ababwa. Later that evening Prince Ali took Jasmine for a ride on his wonderful carpet. The Prince looked very familiar. "Aren't you the boy from the marketplace?" asked Jasmine.

"No, I'm Prince Ali," Aladdin insisted, even though he knew he wasn't being honest.

Then the magic carpet took them back to the palace.

"That was just wonderful," sighed Jasmine. She had fallen in love.

Aladdin was thrilled that things finally seemed to be going his way.

But suddenly the Sultan's guards, under orders from Jafar, appeared and grabbed poor Aladdin. After they tossed him into the sea, Aladdin summoned the Genie and used his second wish to save his own life.

Aladdin returned to the palace with the lamp, but Iago, Jafar's parrot, stole it, and Jafar became the Genie's master.

"Make me Sultan," Jafar commanded.

"And make the Princess and her father my slaves."

The Genie was forced to obey. The poor sultan was hanging from his throne room like a puppet watching

Jafar take over his kingdom. He also had to watch his daughter wait on Jafar's every whim.

Jafar used his second wish to become an all-powerful sorcerer. He changed Aladdin back into a beggar and sent him far away. Aladdin thought he was doomed until the magic carpet appeared and helped him return to the palace. Jafar was furious, but Aladdin found a way to trick him.

"The Genie still has more power than you'll ever have," he told Jafar.

This infuriated Jafar and he used his third wish to become a genie. But he forgot one important thing. Genies become the prisoners of their lamps, shackled to them for all time. Jafar disappeared into a glowing black lamp.

To Jasmine's delight, the Sultan decided to let the

Princess choose her own husband. And there was only one choice for Jasmine—Aladdin.

Now it was Aladdin's turn to make someone happy. He turned to the Genie and said, "I wish for your freedom." And that was the best wish of all!

DISNEY's

THE
LION KING

Everything in the animal kingdom had its place in the circle of life. When the Lion King, Mufasa, and his queen, Sarabi, had a cub named Simba, Mufasa knew that one day Simba would be king. Everyone bowed in respect as Rafiki the baboon introduced the young prince to all the animals.

Only one lion—Mufasa's brother, Scar—refused to attend the ceremony. He was not happy that Simba would be next in line for Mufasa's throne.

But Simba grew into a happy, healthy cub. One day he proudly told his uncle, "Someday I'm going to rule the whole kingdom! Everything except that shadowy place.

I'm not allowed to go there."

"You're absolutely right, Simba," his uncle agreed slyly.

"Only the bravest lions can go to the elephant graveyard."

Scar deliberately tempted his adventurous nephew.

Simba immediately raced home and convinced his

friend Nala to explore the elephant graveyard. It was

creepier than they ever imagined.

Zazu, Mufasa's advisor, caught up with the cubs and warned them it was dangerous, too.

But Simba only laughed at Zazu. Then he heard someone laughing back. He turned to see three enemy hyenas ready for lunch. "He's a king fit for a meal," laughed one.

The nasty hyenas

chased the cubs right into a trap. Suddenly there was a tremendous roar. Mufasa arrived and frightened the hyenas away.

Simba was very proud of his father. "We'll always be together, right?" he asked Mufasa later that evening.

"Look up at the stars, Simba," said Mufasa. "Those are the great kings of the past looking down on us.

Remember those

kings will always be

there to guide you. So

will I."

Although Scar was

very angry with the

hyenas for letting

Simba escape, he made a bargain with them. If they

helped him become king, they could have their run of the

Pride Lands. And Scar had a plan.

Later Scar brought Simba to a gorge and promised

him a wonderful surprise if he would wait on a certain

rock. Then he signaled the hyenas.

The surprise was a stampeding herd of wildebeests!

The earth trembled as the wildebeests headed right

into the gorge and straight toward Simba. Simba

held onto a tree
branch but was
slipping fast.

In an instant
Mufasa appeared
and grabbed his
son. He got Simba

to safety, but then he slipped off the ledge and fell into the thundering stampede.

When everything was quiet once more, Simba found his father lying lifeless at the foot of a cliff. Simba had not seen Scar push Mufasa to his death. Simba believed it was all his fault.

"Run away, Simba," Scar advised the young cub. "Run away and never return."

Scar watched as the young cub ran away, chased by

the hyenas. Then Scar returned to Pride Rock and announced to the lions that he would be their new king.

Simba ended up in the desert, where he collapsed from heat and exhaustion. Luckily two curious creatures found him—a meerkat called Timon and a warthog named Pumbaa.

Simba's new friends took him home to the jungle,

where they introduced him to Timon's idea of hakuna

matata—"no worries."

Simba tried to put the past behind him, but it was

difficult. One day a young lioness appeared, looking for

help. It was Nala.
She told Simba the
sad story of what had
happened since Scar
had taken over the
Pride Lands.

But Simba could
not face going
back—at least not
until Rafiki appeared and led him to a vision of his father.
"You are my son and the one true king. You must take
your place in the circle of life," Mufasa explained.

So Simba returned to the Pride Lands with his friends by his side. There was a great battle. Finally, Scar 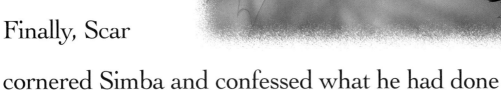 cornered Simba and confessed what he had done many years ago. "You didn't kill your father," Scar said evilly. "I did."

At last Simba found the strength to fight back. He flipped the evil lion right over the edge of the rock into the jaws of the waiting hyenas.

When the fighting was over, Simba took his rightful place as king and restored the Pride Lands to a place of peace. And when Simba and Nala's little cub was born, a brand-new circle of life was begun.

DISNEY'S

POCAHONTAS

One day Pocahontas visited Grandmother Willow, a wise old tree spirit. Pocahontas was confused. Her father wanted her to marry Kocoum, a brave warrior. But Pocahontas did not believe that this was the right path for her. She had dreamed of a spinning arrow and asked Grandmother Willow about the meaning of her dream.

"It is pointing you down your path," she told Pocahontas.

"But how do I find my path?" Pocahontas asked.

"Listen with your heart and you will understand," Grandmother Willow told her. "The spirits are everywhere. They will guide you."

So Pocahontas climbed a tall tree to listen to the wind. Off in the distance she saw strange, billowing clouds.

The clouds Pocahontas thought she saw were really the sails of a large ship. Aboard were men from England coming to the New World in search of gold.

When the ship touched shore, a man called John Smith set out to explore the new land. He met a funny raccoon called Meeko, Pocahontas's friend.

Pocahontas hid from the stranger. But when he heard rustling in the bushes, he knew someone was there. Finally the two stood face-to-face. Pocahontas

was scared; she ran to her canoe to get away. But the stranger called after her. "Don't go! I won't hurt you!"

Pocahontas did not understand what John Smith was saying, but she remembered Grandmother Willow's words. When she listened with her heart, she saw that he was kind. The two quickly became friends.

Meanwhile, at Governor Ratcliffe's orders, John Smith's crew began digging up the new land in search of gold. When the Indians from Pocahontas's tribe approached the settlers, the Governor called them "savages." He ordered his men to draw their guns and fire.

The Indians had never seen weapons like guns before. Powhatan, who was the chief and Pocahontas's father, declared war against these dangerous men.

Back in the forest, Pocahontas and John Smith got acquainted. Ever curious, and always in search of food, Meeko took a compass from John Smith's bag. "What is that?" Pocahontas asked.

"It helps you find your way when you are lost," John Smith explained. "Meeko can keep it. I can buy another one in London."

Pocahontas wanted to hear all about London. John

Smith described the wonders of the city. Then he told Pocahontas that the settlers would build a city like London in the New World. Pocahontas didn't think they needed a city in the middle of her beautiful forest. She decided it was time to introduce John Smith to the wonders of nature all around them.

Pocahontas even took John Smith to meet Grandmother Willow. He was amazed. "One look at this place and the men will forget about digging for gold," Smith said.

"What is gold?" Pocahontas asked.

John Smith showed her a gold coin. Pocahontas told him that there was nothing like this on her land.

John Smith rushed back to his camp to tell Ratcliffe that there was no gold to be found. But the Governor didn't believe him. He thought the Indians wanted to keep it all. And Ratcliffe wanted to take it by force.

When Pocahontas tried to tell her father that they must find a peaceful way to deal with the strangers, Powhatan's braves didn't agree. They wanted to fight. Pocahontas convinced her father that if one of the strangers would come and talk in peace, he must listen.

That night, Pocahontas met John Smith at Grandmother Willow. She convinced him to come with her and talk to her father. But neither she nor John Smith knew that a settler named Thomas was watching them. So was Kocoum. Suddenly Kocoum jumped out of the woods and attacked John Smith. Thomas fired at Kocoum.

"Thomas, run!" Smith cried.

As Thomas fled,

warriors captured Smith.

"At sunrise, this man will die," the chief told his people.

Pocahontas did not know what to do. Suddenly Meeko dropped the compass into her lap. She looked at the needle moving back and forth. "The spinning arrow!" she whispered.

"It's the arrow from your dream showing you your path. Let the spirits guide you," Grandmother Willow said.

Pocahontas ran like the wind. She stopped the

warriors from hurting Smith. The Indians put down their weapons and refused to fight.

But Ratcliffe grabbed a musket and shot at Powhatan. John Smith jumped in front of the chief and took the bullet himself.

The wounded Smith had to return to England. So did the greedy governor, who was now in chains.

As they were about to set sail, Pocahontas and her friend said good-bye. "Come with me?" John Smith asked hopefully.

"I am needed here," Pocahontas replied sadly.

"Then know that wherever I am, I'll always be with you." John Smith smiled as he left.

Pocahontas knew that in their hearts, they would always be together.

DISNEY'S
THE HUNCHBACK OF NOTRE DAME

Long, long ago in the city of Paris, a young, odd-shaped man lived up in the bell tower of the great Cathedral of Notre Dame. He was the bell ringer Quasimodo. His name meant "half-formed," and had been

given to him by his cruel master, Judge Claude Frollo.
Quasimodo's only friends were the stone gargoyles that
came to life in his small world.

Quasimodo longed
to walk in the city
below his tower
prison, but Frollo
forbade it. He was a
mean man who hated
everything and
everyone—especially
gypsies. He had even

convinced gentle Quasimodo that he was a monster, and that terrible things would happen if he went out among the people.

Once a year, all of Paris prepared for a great festival. On that day, known as the Festival of Fools, the people paraded around the city dressed in scary masks and hoped to be crowned the King of Fools. The gargoyles told Quasimodo that this year he must attend the festival.

Everyone was so busy having a grand time, no one noticed the poor bell ringer wandering around. He met the dancing gypsy, Esmeralda, and thought she was beautiful. So did

Phoebus, Frollo's new Captain of the Guard, who rode into Paris that same day.

When Quasimodo was crowned King of Fools, the people laughed. They threw ropes over him to hold him down. Frollo would not rescue Quasimodo, but Esmeralda ran to cut Quasimodo free.

Frollo was enraged. He ordered Phoebus to arrest her.

But Esmeralda and her gray goat, Djali, ran into the cathedral where she knew she would be safe. Frollo's soldiers could not touch her once she was inside. But Frollo warned her, "Set one foot outside these walls, and you're my prisoner!"

Quasimodo did not understand. He believed that all

gypsies were bad, but Esmeralda was good and kind and gentle. His master had been wrong. Maybe Frollo had been wrong about him, too. Maybe he wasn't a monster!

Quasimodo decided to help Esmeralda escape.

Quasimodo carried Esmeralda and Djali down the side of the cathedral. When they got to the street, she gave him a special amulet to keep. "Use this if you ever need help," she explained. "It will lead you to the Court of Miracles, where you can find me." Then, promising to visit him soon, Esmeralda vanished.

Meanwhile, Phoebus convinced Esmeralda that he

was on her side—not Frollo's. When Phoebus refused to do the judge's bidding, Frollo turned on the Captain and ordered his soldiers to kill him. The injured Phoebus managed to escape with Esmeralda's

help. She took him to Quasimodo in the bell tower and asked him to hide Phoebus for her.

Quasimodo sadly agreed, for he could see that the two

were in love. Soon Frollo came to the bell tower, hoping

to trick Quasimodo into telling him where Esmeralda was

hiding. He convinced Quasimodo that he already knew

about the gypsies'

hideout, the Court of

Miracles, and planned

to attack at dawn.

Quasimodo and

Phoebus set out to

warn Esmeralda

about Frollo's plans.

Using the amulet,

they found their way to the Court of Miracles. They did not realize something very important: They were leading Frollo and his soldiers there, as well.

"Take them away!" Frollo cried. They were all his prisoners now.

But chains could not hold the determined bell ringer. Quasimodo escaped and rescued

Esmeralda. Phoebus, the gypsies, Quasimodo, and the gargoyles fought bravely against Frollo and his soldiers. When the battle was over, the trio walked out of the cathedral and into the sunlight smiling. Quasimodo was cheered by the crowd. The bell ringer who once thought he was a monster was now a great hero!

DISNEY'S

HERCULES

Long ago, a mighty god named Zeus locked the monstrous Titans away so that he and his gods and goddesses could rule the world from Mount Olympus.

One day, Zeus's wife, Hera, gave birth to a bouncing baby boy. All the gods gathered to celebrate his birthday.

His name was Hercules and his gift was strength. The proud father presented the baby with a flying horse called Pegasus.

There was one god who was especially unhappy with Zeus. He was Hades, the god of the Underworld. Hades had a plan to take over Olympus and make Zeus his prisoner. When the time was right, he planned to unleash the Titans. But he wanted to make sure that things would go according to his plan.

Hades asked the Fates—three sisters who shared one eye and could see into the future. They told Hades that he would defeat Zeus in eighteen years when the planets lined up—as long as Hercules did not fight. If he did,

Hades would fail.

Hades decided to get rid of little Hercules. He knew that he could if Hercules were

mortal. So the god of the Underworld sent his henchmen, Pain and Panic, to steal the baby and feed him a potion that would make him human.

Before Hercules could finish the bottle, Pain and Panic were interrupted by a kind older couple—Amphitryon and Alcmene—who rescued the baby and raised him as their own.

As Hercules grew into a teenager, he was strong but clumsy. He was always in trouble with the other boys and villagers. Hercules tried to fit in, but something always happened, and he ended up causing a lot of destruction. Hercules just knew he didn't belong.

Finally, Hercules' parents decided to tell him how they found him as a baby. He had been wearing a gold medallion that was a symbol of the gods. Hercules believed that the gods held the answer to his past. So he went to Zeus's temple to find out.

In the temple, the statue of Zeus came alive. Zeus explained that Hercules was his son, and that if the boy could prove himself a true hero on Earth, he would be a god again. Then he could come home to Mount Olympus. Zeus sent Hercules to find Philoctetes, who knew how to train heroes.

Hercules found Phil and trained hard. Phil believed that Hercules was ready to be a hero. So he took him to Thebes. On the way, Hercules rescued a woman named Megara from a centaur and fell in love. He didn't know that Meg was working for Hades.

Hades tried to get rid of Hercules by forcing him to

battle the Hydra—a monster with many heads. But

Hercules won!

So Hades sent Meg to find Hercules' weakness.

Meg fell in love with him and didn't want anything

to happen to Hercules.

When Hades realized the two were in love, he told Hercules that unless he gave up his strength for twenty-four hours, Meg would get hurt. Hercules agreed, but only if Meg would be safe. Hades gave him his promise.

Hades' plan was in place. With Hercules out of the way, it was time to unleash the Titans. Hades sent all but one after Zeus. He saved the Cyclops for Hercules. The Cyclops headed for Thebes to destroy Hercules and the city. Hercules battled the one-eyed monster and defeated him. But when Hercules stood in front of a damaged column that was about to fall, Meg pushed him out of the way. The pillar fell on Meg and crushed her.

Hades' deal was broken instantly! Hercules regained his strength and headed for Mount Olympus to stop the

evil god. He freed everyone and defeated the Titans. But Hades still had Meg. Hercules headed down to the Underworld to save her. Hades watched gleefully as Hercules dived into the Pit of Souls. He knew that no mortal ever came out. But Hercules had at last proved that he was a true hero. He was a god once more, and he climbed out of the pit with Meg safe and sound.

Now Hercules could come home to the gods on Mount Olympus. But something was stopping him. In the end, Hercules knew where he belonged—on Earth with Meg.

Walt Disney's

MICKEY
and the
BEANSTALK

ong, long ago, there was a place where the sun smiled all day. It was called Happy Valley. Everything in Happy Valley was pretty and green and...happy. The people who lived there were happy, too.

High on a hilltop overlooking this sweet little place stood a beautiful castle. In the castle lived a golden harp

who sang the day away. The harp had Happy Valley under her very happy spell.

Then one day a terribly sad thing

happened. Someone stole the golden harp from the castle and broke the magic spell. Everything stopped working and growing. And everyone stopped feeling happy. Soon there was nothing to eat, and the people grew sad and hungry.

Three farmers decided there was nothing left to do but sell their cow. Mickey took Bossy into town. When he returned, he showed Donald and Goofy the three beans he'd gotten for the cow.

"Three beans!" cried his friends. "We can't live on three beans!" Donald grabbed the beans and threw them on the floor.

"But…but…they are magic beans," Mickey tried to explain as he sadly watched the beans roll through a crack in the floor.

During the night, under the very bright moonlight, the

beans began to grow. They grew into a huge stalk that climbed all the way to the sky, carrying the farmers' little house with it.

When the hungry farmers awoke, they looked out the window. Happy Valley was gone. All they could see from the beanstalk was a very big castle and a lot of fluffy clouds.

"Let's go!" cried Mickey. "Whoever lives in that big castle must have plenty of food. Maybe he'll share!"

Sure enough, when they crept inside the castle, they saw huge bowls and plates filled with food. As they finished eating, they heard a tiny voice call out to them from a box on the table.

"Who are you?" Mickey, Donald, and Goofy asked.

"It is I, the golden harp," said the tiny voice. "A giant stole me and brought me here to sing for him."

The farmers were very frightened when the heard the word "giant." They almost ran away immediately. But Mickey reminded them that they couldn't leave without the magic harp.

"We have to rescue her and save Happy Valley!" Goofy said.

Just then everything in the room started shaking. Somebody as big as a giant was coming! Mickey, Donald, and Goofy ran and hid.

The giant walked over to the table and made himself a sandwich. He was just about to take a bite when he noticed Mickey wriggling around.

"Run!" Mickey shouted to Donald and Goofy.

The giant was very angry. He chased them around the room until he had two of them cornered. Then the giant put Donald and Goofy into the box with the golden harp, locked it, and slipped the key into his pocket.

Mickey hid quietly until the giant fell asleep. Then he tiptoed over to the box and knocked.

"Get the key out of his pocket," the golden harp whispered.

Ever so carefully, Mickey did just that. The giant

stirred in his sleep, but he didn't wake up.

Mickey let his friends and the harp out of the box.

Quietly, they made their way to the front door of the

castle. But just as they were sneaking past the giant, he

opened one eye and

saw them! What a

roar they heard!

Mickey decided

to distract the giant

so his friends could

get the harp to

safety. He teased the giant, who chased him all over the castle. Finally Mickey jumped out an open window and

ran over to the beanstalk. He slid down after his friends.

Donald and Goofy grabbed a saw and began to cut down the beanstalk. The giant kept climbing down, down, down. When the beanstalk fell, he crashed right through the ground!

The farmers took the golden harp back to her castle on the hilltop, where she could sing once more. And Happy Valley was once again a very happy place.

WALT DISNEY'S

THREE LITTLE PIGS

Once upon a time, there were three little pigs who went out into the world to build their homes and seek their fortunes.

The first little pig did not like to work at all. He quickly built his house of straw because that was the easiest way. Then he danced off down the road to see how his brothers were getting along.

The second little pig was building himself a house, too. He did not like to work either, so he decided to build his house out of sticks. That would be quick and easy. Soon he was finished. The house made of sticks was not very strong, but at least his work was done. Now he was free to play.

What the second little pig

liked to do best was play his fiddle. The first little pig

played his flute while his brother played the fiddle and

danced. Then the two went off down the road to see

about their brother.

The third little pig was the serious one. He was

building his house out of bricks. He did not mind

working hard, and he
wanted his house to be
strong. For he knew that
in the woods nearby lived
a big, bad wolf who liked
nothing better than to
catch little pigs and eat
them! So he worked and

worked, putting each and every brick carefully in place.

The first two pigs laughed when they saw their brother
hard at work. But the third little pig just ignored them
and went about building his house. "You can laugh and

dance and sing," he called after his brothers. "But I'll be safe and you'll be sorry when the wolf comes to the door!"

The first pig had just reached his house of straw when the wolf came knocking at his door.

"Little pig, little pig, let me come in!" cried the wolf.

"Not by the hair of my chinny-chin-chin!" said the little pig.

"Then I'll huff and I'll puff and I'll blow your house in!" roared the wolf.

And he did. Why, he blew the little straw house all to pieces!

The poor little pig ran off to his brother's house made of sticks. But there was the wolf waiting for him. He knew that the pigs would not let him inside, so he disguised himself as a sheep. Luckily the pigs could see through the wolf's disguise.

"You can't fool us with that sheepskin!" cried the pigs.

"Then I'll huff and I'll puff, and I'll blow your house

in!" yelled the wolf.

And he blew the little house of twigs all to pieces!

The two pigs raced off to their brother's brick house.

"Don't worry," said the third little pig. "You are safe here."

Soon they were laughing and singing again.

This made the wolf very angry. He huffed and he puffed and he puffed and he huffed. But no matter how hard he tried, he could not blow down that little house of bricks.

The wolf thought and thought about how to get inside.

Ah-ha! He could climb down the chimney. And so he did,

right into a bubbling kettle of water that the pigs had

hung in the fireplace.

With a yelp and a scream, the big, bad wolf flew

straight up the chimney and ran off into the woods. The three little pigs never saw him again. They were most content to sing and laugh and dance inside their brother's strong brick house.